Santa's Gift

Gale Nemec

Drawings by

You! Print your name on this line.

_____

This book belongs to

_____

This book is from

_____

Today's date

_____

You have a *One-of-A-Kind Brain!*

Read this book or listen to someone read it to you. When an idea comes into your *One-of-a-Kind Brain*, you can draw it in this book or on paper. Write the date on your picture so you will remember when you drew it.

Inspired by 4-year-old, Taylor Doremus

One fall day, Taylor and I took a walk, and picked up yellow, red, brown, orange, and green fall leaves. A few of the leaves were two colors. When we got home Taylor found a brown piece of paper and, using her memory, her imagination, and her *One-of-a-Kind Brain*, she cut out a thick tree trunk. It looked like the trees we had seen on our walk. She got a second piece of paper and glued the tree trunk onto it. Next, she glued the leaves she'd picked up to the top of her tree trunk and created a fall tree on paper! It looked like a real tree with different colored leaves. I was so impressed that it inspired me to write *Santa's Gift*.

God has given you a *One-of-a-Kind Brain*. No one has a brain like yours, no two brains are the same. Creating and making art is one of the things you can do with *YOUR One-of-a-Kind Brain*. You can sing, draw, dance, build, invent, make things, tell jokes, calculate numbers, write stories or poems, clean up, give hugs, and tell someone the ideas that come to you.

Cover by

Dawn LeGros
Sharing is Caring

ISBN 978-1-947608-28-3

Gale B. Nemec
Nemec LLC
Alexandria, Virginia
Copyright © 2024-2025

I wrote a letter to Santa Claus
and one to Mrs. Claus, too!
Because I thought
sending a letter
to the North Pole...
would be better
if I sent two.

I was so disappointed
on that Christmas Day,
but I realized something
that will not go away.

Santa said "No."
He didn't give me a lot.
But he gave me a gift. . .
I thought he forgot!

He gave me love!
He gave me joy!
He gave me insight,
Is that better than a toy?

Nothing to play with?
Nothing to do?
"Oh, Santa!
You made me cry!"
Bu-hu-hu-huu!

I wanted a toy!
A toy that might break,
someone might take
or might end up
in some deep lake!

Oh. . .!

. . .was I mad!
And gee! Was I sad!
I felt really, really, really
really, bad.

I whaled! I cried!
I stomped my feet!
"Hey! Santa, you are mean!
You are so mean to me!"

Suddenly a thought
Came into my brain.
I have no idea
from where it came.

"Think of Jesus,
He had nothing at all.
And for heaven's sake
He was born in a stall.

Surrounded by animals
and all kinds of hay.
It didn't smell good
on that miracle day.

As a kid he built things
and worked with his dad.
They built things from wood
and made people glad.

Created! Designed!
Invented things, too.
Tables and chairs!
And they
didn't
have
glue."

"Hummm," I thought,
"I can make
things, too.
Games and toys,
with paper and glue.

Or sticks and sand
or leaves filled with color.
Things I can play with
or give to another."

Santa said, "No,"
so, I could see,
there are things
I can make,
things I can create.

I'll start right now.
I won't hesitate!

I will use
My One-of-a-Kind Brain
No brain like mine!
None are the same.

("Wow. Impressive. . .")

Suddenly I realized. . .

. . .Even though
I did not get a lot,
I have a brain,
believe it or not!

When Santa says "No,"
and you don't get
what you want
Give yourself a hug.
And know...
With your
One-of-a-Kind Brain...
...well...
You have a lot!

The End

Draw, write or think about something you can do with your *One-of-a-Kind-Brain.* Upload it, and share it with me at: Gale@GaleNemecBooks.com

Search Gale Nemec online for
Books, E-books, and Audible Books
Motivate. Create. Educate.

www.GaleNemecBooks.com
Email: Gale@GaleNemecBooks.com

Books by Gale
Little Stockey & The Miracle of Christmas
There's A Bear on A Bench
The Great Elephant Rescue
Throwing Rocks in the River
No Valentines for Trevor or Emily
Valentines for Valentines Day
Trevor and the T's
Andy's Adventurous Nightmare
A Window into Heaven
Hugs
Hugs Two, photo memory book
Benjamin Loves the Beach
Santa's Gift drawing book for boys
Santa's Gift drawing book for girls
A Wish for You
God Held Your Hand

Bilingual: English Spanish
Hay un Oso En La Banca
(There's a Bear on A Bench)

El Pequeño Stockey y el Milagro de la Navidad
(Little Stockey & the Miracle of Christmas)

Non-Fiction
Caught in the Crosshairs of War

You Tube Channel Gale Nemec
Your Song-The Ten Commandments Song

Interact with Gale as she reads!

There's a Bear on a Bench
Throwing Rocks in the River

Please visit. Listen, like and share.

Thank you for reading and buying this book. Please tell the world what you think about it and rate it on Amazon, Good Reads, Google, Facebook, Instagram, X and where you bought it with a star value or a written review. Thank you.

About the Author

Gale Nemec loves to write books that motivate to create and educate its readers. It amazes her when a story starts to form in her *One-of-a-Kind Brian*. A-line-at-time, a story pops into her *One-of-a-Kind Brain*. Sometimes, a story comes so fast she can hardly write it down – and yep - she always writes first on paper and not on a computer. She wrote, *"There's a Bear on a Bench* on scrap paper and *The Great Elephant Rescue* on a small paper napkin!

Gale has written more than a dozen children's fiction books and one non-fiction book, *Caught in the Crosshairs of War*. It is her eyewitness account of Prague Spring in Czechoslovakia. Her fiction books are educational in nature and may introduce numbers or rhyming or encourage creativity through drawing and imagination. Gale received her undergraduate and her master's degree in education at the University of Georgia with an emphasis on Gifted Education. She received the prestigious *Professional Achievement Award* from the University of Georga.

Gale is an award-winning producer, actress, and voice talent. She is also a print model and song writer. She teaches and coaches acting to kids and adults. Her most recent song *Your Song - The Ten Commandment Song* is on her YouTube channel Gale Nemec, and on streaming platforms. She created and Produced *The Bea & the Bug* an award winning, multimedia, interactive musical show featuring American history. Currently, she is creating a web series, *Adventures in Time*, a time-travel series for kids; It is based on *The Bea & The Bug*.

Back cover photo
Athelia Jordan

25

Made in the USA
Middletown, DE
01 March 2025

72044564R00015